BY ALI BOVIS    ILLUSTRATED BY JEN TAYLOR

# SYLVIE
## Sea View Star

Calico

n Imprint of Magic Wagon
abdobooks.com

FOR MATTIE AND JACK,
MY STARS, DREAM BIG,
BELIEVE IN YOURSELF,
AND ENJOY THE
JOURNEY. —AB

FOR MARC AND
MY FAMILY. —JT

abdobooks.com

Published by Magic Wagon, a division of ABDO, PO Box 398166, Minneapolis, Minnesota 55439. Copyright © 2020 by Abdo Consulting Group, Inc. International copyrights reserved in all countries. No part of this book may be reproduced in any form without written permission from the publisher. Calico™ is a trademark and logo of Magic Wagon.

Printed in the United States of America, North Mankato, Minnesota.
092019
012020

THIS BOOK CONTAINS
RECYCLED MATERIALS

Written by Ali Bovis
Illustrated by Jen Taylor
Edited by Bridget O'Brien
Art Directed by Candice Keimig

Library of Congress Control Number: 2019942287

Publisher's Cataloging-in-Publication Data

Names: Bovis, Ali, author. | Taylor, Jen, illustrator.
Title: Sea view star / by Ali Bovis ; illustrated by Jen Taylor.
Description: Minneapolis, Minnesota : Magic Wagon, 2020. | Series: Sylvie; book 1
Summary: Sylvie can't wait to raise money for the animal shelter for her Make a Difference Day project, but with her frenemy, Camilla, and Sylvie's foster puppy creating obstacles along the way, she discovers there is more than one way to make a difference.
Identifiers: ISBN 9781532136511 (lib. bdg.) | ISBN 9781644943199 (pbk.) | ISBN 9781532137112 (ebook) | ISBN 9781532137419 (Read-to-Me ebook)
Subjects: LCSH: Animal shelters--Juvenile fiction. | Puppies--Juvenile fiction. | Fund raising--Juvenile fiction. | Team work in fund raising--Juvenile fiction. | Self-assurance--Juvenile fiction. | Friendship--Juvenile fiction.
Classification: DDC [Fic]--dc23

# TABLE OF CONTENTS

# THE BIG NEWS

Sylvie did not mean to knock Ms. Martin's papers onto the floor. Or Nick's pencil case. Or Camilla's puffball charm. OK, maybe the puffball charm was no accident.

Sylvie was simply too excited to slow down for anything. She had to get to that sign-up sheet first.

Sylvie peeked over her shoulder and examined the wreckage.

Yikes! She had better clean that up, quick!

She doubled back and picked up the papers, the pencil case, and even the puffball charm.

"Thank you," said Sylvie's teacher, Ms. Martin.

"Thanks," said Nick, flashing Sylvie a smile.

Camilla just raised an eyebrow and shook her head. Classic Camilla.

Then, like an Olympic swimmer shoving off the pool mid-race, Sylvie bolted back to the sign-up sheet.

Just in time! The sign-up sheet hung from the clipboard, still blank. But how could that be? Had Sylvie been the only one paying attention during morning announcements? Was she the only one who had heard the big news?

Sylvie surveyed the classroom. Her best friend, Sammy, inspected a dead bug on his bag. Tori twirled her hair. And Camilla was getting a head start on her fractions homework.

*Really?* thought Sylvie. *C'mon, people!*

Josh walked past the sign-up sheet and studied the lunch calendar.

He hurried back to his desk. "Taco Tuesday!" he cheered, high-fiving his twin brother, Nick.

Taco Tuesday? *That's* what he was excited about?

He had missed the announcement. They all had.

At least Sylvie could sign up before anyone else. She looked at her gnawed pencil and the dried doggie drool that crinkled the corners of her notebook.

She thought of her foster puppy and giggled. She had no doubt what her project should be.

Sylvie wrote her name on the top line. Next to it, her project: *help animals*.

She stepped aside and admired her best cursive. "Stellar!" she said.

Sylvie strutted to her seat and tightened her star-speckled hair ribbon. Her mind raced.

She flipped ahead in her planner and jotted a note: *Make a Difference Day*. She circled Saturday, October 26, and doodled stars all around it.

Ms. Martin sat at her desk, reorganizing papers. She straightened her picture frame. Sylvie smiled, and her teacher smiled back.

Sylvie loved Ms. Martin. She shared a name with one of Sylvie's favorite heroes (Dr. Martin Luther King Jr). She also had the most fabulous taste in fashion!

Yep, Sylvie loved her teacher and knew Ms. Martin felt the same way. At the parent-teacher open house, Ms. Martin had told Sylvie's parents that Sylvie was "really something."

Ms. Martin walked past decorations of watercolor witches and tissue paper pumpkins before stopping by the board.

"Thanks for getting us started with the sign-up sheet, Sylvie," she said. "Anyone else? Principal Close would like all of third grade to participate."

"I'm in!" said Nick. "Taco Tuesday is awesome."

Across the room, heads turned. Hands shot up. "Me too!"

"Yum!"

"I also love Taco Tuesday," said Ms. Martin. "But that's not what I'm talking about. Principal Close made another big announcement."

The class grew quiet.

"The book fair?" asked Camilla.

"School carnival?" asked Tori.

"Snow day!" Josh and Nick cheered together.

Sylvie's eyes popped wider than an endangered spotted owl's. How could they have missed Principal Close's announcement? How could they have missed the BIG NEWS? And how could there be a snow day in October—in Southern California?

Sylvie shook her head so much that she felt like one of her endangered animals bobblehead toys.

She tried to get Sammy's attention. She cleared her throat. She tapped her foot. She rocked her chair. No luck.

*Ugh! He's usually such a good listener,* Sylvie thought.

Sammy gently poked the dead bug on his bag. He nudged the dead bug.

He . . . *saved the dead bug?* Sylvie wondered, as it fluttered its wings.

Ms. Martin grabbed the clipboard with the sign-up sheet. "Principal Close made an announcement about Make a Difference Day," she said.

Sylvie tipped her chair forward.

"It's in one week," Ms. Martin went on. "It's a special day across the country when everyone comes together to help others."

Sylvie blurted, "Everyone gets to pick a project and volunteer. Everyone can make a difference and change the world. And there'll be lunch with the mayor! It's so stellar!"

"That's right," said Ms. Martin. "All students who participate get extra credit. Plus a pizza party with Mayor Flores."

Suddenly all eyes were on Ms. Martin. The room fell silent. Tori stopped twirling her hair.

"Pizza?" asked Josh, nudging Nick.

"Extra credit?" asked Camilla.

Even Sammy paid attention. The no-longer-dead bug skittered away.

All at once, the class made a mad dash for the sign-up sheet. Papers, pencil cases, and puffball charms fell to the floor. Some kids pushed. Others shoved.

In no time, the paper filled up with every last name in the class. *Finally. Everyone is showing the appropriate level of enthusiasm,* thought Sylvie.

Now everyone wanted to make a difference. Or eat pizza. Sylvie didn't know which. It didn't matter.

She felt certain her plan to help all the animals in the world would make the biggest difference of all. Just as soon as she figured out how!

# HELP THE ANIMALS!

Outside, third graders swarmed around the benches, talking about Make a Difference Day. Almost the entire grade had signed on. Everyone wanted the scoop on what projects other kids were planning.

A boy pledged to save the rain forests. All of them!

A girl pledged to save the whales. All of them!

Principal Close pledged to order toppings on the pizzas. All of them!

Sylvie joined Sammy in the car line. Back in the classroom, Sylvie was glad to see Sammy sign up to help animals. Which made sense, since Sammy was *the* animal expert of third grade.

"Sammy," she announced as they got into her dad's car, "we've got our work cut out for us."

At home, Sylvie tossed her things on a chair in the backyard. Sammy put his backpack next to hers and started digging for bugs.

He was not the only one. Sylvie's foster puppy was a great digger. *Maybe too great,* Sylvie thought. The lawn was starting to look like Swiss cheese!

Sylvie gave the dog a big hug. The dog barked. He slobbered on Sylvie and trotted off. That silly, slobbery dog!

Sylvie was so happy her parents had agreed to watch him until the animal shelter had room. When the Schwartzes found him, he had no collar and was starving.

Sure, he could be "a bit much," as Sylvie's neighbor, Mr. Wolf, had said.

But that didn't matter. Sylvie thought he was cute. Anyway, it was only for a little while, until the shelter picked him up next weekend.

Sylvie tapped Sammy's shoulder and pointed to the swing set. They always got their best ideas on the swings. "Race you up!" She hopped on a swing and pumped her legs. Sammy followed.

Sylvie tightened her grip and kicked in the air. "We need to do something extra stellar for the animals."

"Sure," he replied, pumping high. "What?"

Sylvie pondered. Then, from the top of her swing, she spotted something in the yard next door. Camilla's yard. Her legs froze. "Sammy," she whispered.

"Yeah?" Sammy whispered back.

"Camilla's out in her yard." Why was she wearing a glittery pink gardening outfit? And carrying a pink rake? Most of all, what was she doing with those leaves? "I wonder what she's up to."

Sylvie knew Camilla would do anything for extra credit. The leaves must have something to do with her Make a Difference Day project.

Whatever Camilla was doing, Sylvie was glad she was making a difference. The world needed all the help it could get! Still, she couldn't help hoping her project would be better.

She hopped off her swing, got her backpack, and pulled out her list. "What

if we create an Animal Extravaganza with dancing parrots and acrobatic beetles? The money raised could be donated to animal organizations."

The dog did some acrobatic moves of his own. Then he launched after a squirrel.

"Hmm." Sammy tilted his head. "I have a few ideas too. Maybe we can look over our lists together."

Sylvie knew Sammy would be full of awesome ideas. Sammy slowed his swing and pulled out a piece of paper. He passed it to Sylvie.

"An art show to raise money for animals?" asked Sylvie, waving her list. "I had the same idea! Here, number 139."

"Number 139?" asked Sammy, his mouth opened wide.

Just then, a scream rang out from past the trees.

Sylvie turned. She'd recognize that scream anywhere. And after, Sylvie heard a very familiar bark.

The art show for animals would have to wait. An explosion of leaves swirled in the air. Sylvie dropped the lists, grabbed the dog's leash, and sprinted to the yard next door.

# LEAVES, LEAVES, EVERYWHERE!

"Uh-oh," Sylvie whispered.

The dog rolled over and barked. Bits of plastic dangled from his mouth.

Sylvie peered around Camilla's yard. Leaves, leaves, everywhere!

Sylvie trudged through the foliage. She kicked up shredded plastic garbage bags, cookie crumbs on an otherwise-empty plate, and a drooled-on hot pink rake.

Yikes! This was not good. Her foster pup had destroyed Camilla's bags of leaves—and eaten her snack. Camilla was going to be so mad.

Sylvie patted her knee. "Come here, boy," she called. The dog galloped over and knocked Sylvie down. Sylvie got up and clipped his leash to his collar.

"That dog!" huffed Camilla.

Sylvie noticed Camilla was wearing her "Student of the Week" pin. Again. It was fastened where the matching "best friends" pin she and Sylvie shared used to go.

"I'm really sorry, Camilla," Sylvie said.

Camilla pinched up her face and pulled a twig out of her hair. "Leaf collecting can make a person thirsty," she said. "I went inside to make some of my world-famous lemonade. Look at what he did!"

The dog barked. He wagged his tail. He rolled over.

Camilla shook her head.

Sylvie petted the dog. She turned to her former lemonade stand business partner. "Sorry, again. He really didn't mean it. He chews on my things all the time. My breakfast, my lunch. He almost got my retainer!"

Camilla swirled crushed ice in her cup. She smacked her lips and glared at Sylvie. "Well, don't let it happen again. Keep him away from my leaves. My cookies. And my everything else!"

"OK," Sylvie said. She scanned the yard. "I'll get another rake and more bags. I can clean this up."

For some reason, Camilla didn't like the sound of that. She picked up her rake and wiped the slobber off.

"No, no," she said. "I was practicing for Make a Difference Day. I don't want help."

"Practicing?" asked Sylvie.

Camilla opened a new bag and stuffed leaves inside. "That's right. I'm going to clean up all of Ms. Kay's leaves because she'll be away."

So *that* was Camilla's plan. Sylvie had to admit, Camilla picked a great project.

Everyone loved Ms. Kay. She gave out full-sized candy bars on Halloween, books on birthdays, and most exciting of all, Ms. Kay volunteered at city hall.

In the mail room! She was a big deal. It meant a lot to have a VIP like her on their block.

Sylvie and Sammy needed to get to work! "OK. See you later," said Sylvie. She tugged the dog's leash. "And let me know if you change your mind about the leaves."

Camilla went back to raking. Sylvie and the dog ran home faster than either had ever run before.

Sammy was in the kitchen eating snickerdoodles with Sylvie's younger brother, Henry. Sylvie grabbed one and tossed it to the puppy. They were his favorite.

"Ready to start planning our art show for animals?" asked Sylvie. "Or 'Paint Out!' Sounds more stellar, doesn't it?"

"Wait. What?" asked Sammy.

"The Paint Out. We can have it on Beach Street. People can paint portraits of their pets outside the shops. Then we can sell the paintings. We can donate the money to the Sea View Animal Shelter."

"They could help all the animals in Sea View," said Sammy.

"Perfect! I bet we can help all the animals in Sea View, and all of the animals in all of the world!" Sylvie said. "Then possibly one day, we can organize an expedition to space, to see if any animals need help there, too."

Sammy didn't have anything to say after that. Clearly he was as excited as Sylvie.

They got to work right away. Before dinner, they had gotten permission from the town to hold the Paint Out, informed the Sea View Animal Shelter of their upcoming "biggest donation ever," and told friends and family to save the date.

Sylvie was relieved that her and Sammy's plan was underway. But she soon felt worried again.

Sure, she and Sammy and Camilla had come up with stellar projects. But what about everyone else in their class? Had they picked their projects, too?

# PLANNING PARTY HEADQUARTERS

The next morning, bags and boxes shifted with the car's every turn. Poster boards in twine rustled on the roof. The ride to school felt like it wouldn't end.

"Can you drive faster, Mom?" asked Sylvie, a tickle forming in her nose. *Don't sneeze*, she thought. *Don't even think about sneezing!*

"My toes hurt!" Henry whined. "And I can't reach my snack."

Sylvie guessed the box of binders was weighing on her brother's feet. She tried to turn her head to see. No use.

"What's that, kids?" Sylvie's mom asked.

A clipboard slammed into Sylvie's side. She reminded herself this was all for the big day.

"Oh, nothing. We're OK," she said. "I put a few extra things in the car today. It's for the projects I told you and Dad about last night."

"Yes," said Sylvie's mom, chuckling. "I noticed a *few* extra things."

When Sylvie called around to her tell friends about the Paint Out, she learned they had stellar project ideas too. She figured they would need her help. She looked over her list.

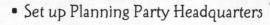

- Set up Planning Party Headquarters

- Give stationary to Lila and Zaki for cards for soldiers

- Give seeds to Tori and Lori for community garden

- Give gift wrap to Malik and Omeed for toys for kids in the hospital

- Give poster boards to Josh and Nick for free hugs signs

- Give garbage bags to Camilla for leaf cleanup (Maybe!)

At school, Sylvie, Henry, and their mom helped unload. After only six trips, they had carried the supplies into Ms. Martin's classroom.

Sylvie wanted to rename it the Planning Party Headquarters. Ms. Martin had said they'd have to stick with calling it Class 307, but she liked how Sylvie thought.

Sylvie pulled a cotton cobweb off the clock. Five minutes until morning announcements.

Ms. Martin had agreed to give Sylvie time to speak. Sylvie went in front of the class and turned up the volume on her megaphone. "Welcome to Planning Party Headquarters," she announced. "Let's do this!"

"Planning Party Headquarters?" asked Camilla, rolling her eyes.

"Yep." Sylvie ignored her. "We can help each other plan our projects. There's power in numbers, people."

"Awesome!" said Josh. Everyone else in Class 307 seemed to agree.

Before long, the imagination station was covered in construction paper and crayons. The book nook became a bonanza of binders, clipboards, and tape.

Sammy helped give out the items Sylvie had brought.

"Sylvie!" called Josh, waving a poster board.

"Check out our signs," said Nick.

Sylvie held up a "Free Hugs!" poster, examining it from every angle. "Terrific start. For the rest, you might want to rethink the whole print thing. Cursive can really spruce up a poster."

Walking back to her desk, Sylvie stubbed her toe on a box. *Ouch!* What

was in there, anyway? She poked her hand in and felt soft plastic. Of course. The garbage bags for Camilla.

Sylvie sighed. "Ms. Martin, do you know where Camilla went?"

"She ran to the bathroom," answered her teacher. "She thinks she might have left her honor roll bracelet there."

Her honor roll bracelet, of course. For a moment, Sylvie wondered if she should even help Camilla.

What if Camilla cleaned up so many leaves she outshined everyone else?

Sylvie pictured Camilla perched on top of a mountain of garbage bags bursting with Ms. Kay's leaves. She'd name it Mount Camilla, and everyone would gather to see it.

But then Sylvie remembered the project sign-up sheet. Everyone had partnered up. Everyone except Camilla. That was how she usually operated.

"I want to ride alone," Camilla had said on the seesaw last week. But she didn't look happy then. She probably wasn't now either.

Before Sylvie could talk herself out of it, she stuffed her extra garbage bags into Camilla's backpack. Then she sprinted back to her seat.

Make a Difference Day was only six days away. Sylvie had more important things to worry about like paint, glitter, glue, and sprinkles. And, helping all the animals in the world! Then there was the matter of finding a spaceship.

# MAKE A DIFFERENCE DAY MORNING

The sun's rays peeked through the darkness. Landscape lights turned off. Sprinklers switched on.

With all that planning, the week had flown by. The paint, glitter, glue, and sprinkles were gathered, ready to decorate the blank canvases. Make a Difference Day was finally here!

Sylvie heard a knock at the door. She jumped. More knocks. This time there were four. Three soft and one loud: Sammy's special knock.

How could it be 6:15 in the morning already? Sylvie flung the door open and pulled her best friend inside.

"Sammy, thank goodness. It's getting late!"

Sammy looked at the clock. He made a confused face. "OK, we're ready. Mom and Dad squeezed in the supplies you brought over yesterday into the car. And the booth for the dog."

A smile spread across Sylvie's face. "Ah, yes! You mean the booth for my

Make a Difference Day star! He'll sit in his booth for everyone to see, admire, and even paint!"

Sammy picked up the new boxes Sylvie had set out. "That sounds great," he said. He pointed to the photo album on top of the boxes. "I brought some pictures of my pets that people can use as models."

"Stellar!" said Sylvie. Who wouldn't want to browse through Sammy's album of pets for inspiration?

Sylvie ran upstairs and switched on her megaphone. "Mom, Dad, Henry, my Make a Difference Day star! Time to go!"

A loud crash echoed through the house. Was it people jumping out of bed? Or falling in the dark? Suddenly, the dog flew down the steps and darted out the door.

Hmm, what possibly could have caused all that noise? She would figure it out later.

Sylvie lowered the volume on her megaphone. "I've got the dog. We'll head over to the Paint Out with Sammy. See you there!"

For a second time that week, Sylvie and the puppy ran faster than they ever had.

Two hours later, Sylvie put down her glue and took in their work. She and Sammy had transformed Beach Street into the biggest Paint Out party in the history of Sea View.

Sylvie looked around. A balloon arch spelled "Happy Make a Difference Day" from streetlight to streetlight. Paint-themed songs blasted over speakers.

Blank canvases lined the street from Sea View Slices to Sea View Scoops, and everything in between. Paint cans and buckets of brushes were set out on a big table. Bowls of glitter, glue, and decorative rainbow sprinkles sparkled in the morning light.

People arrived by foot, car, and bus. And an occasional surfboard.

When Sylvie's family got there, she put them into position.

Sammy flipped his photo album to a picture of his bearded dragon and turtle. "I think we're ready," he said.

"Just a few finishing touches," Sylvie said. She ran to the booth and fluffed the dog's pillows. She wiped drool off his jowls. She colored chalk stars on the street around him.

"Now?" Sammy asked.

Sylvie nodded. She squeezed in a few warm-up stretches and reached for her megaphone. "Places, people! We're open for business. Let the Paint Out begin!"

# PAINT OUT!

Mr. Wolf was their first customer. He walked up to the table. "Alright, kids. Tell me how this works."

Sammy handed him a canvas and brush. "Glitter, glue, and decorative rainbow sprinkles are on the table," Sylvie said. "All you need to do is paint a picture of your favorite pet or animal."

"At the end of the day, we'll sell the paintings and donate the money to the

Sea View Animal Shelter," explained Sammy. Mr. Wolf smiled.

"That's right!" Sylvie went on. "We'll make enough money to help all the animals of Sea View, and the entire world. Then of course there's the matter of the space animals."

Mr. Wolf's forehead scrunched up. His eyebrows looked funny. He must've been concentrating on thinking up a design.

"Alright," he said. "Let's help all the animals of the world and then the space animals?"

A smile spread across Sylvie's face. "You got it!"

Before long, the Paint Out was in full swing. Empty canvases filled with color. Rainbows swirled in water jars as paintbrushes were rinsed. Dogs, cats, hamsters, and even a rat adorned the art of Sea View's citizens.

Sylvie checked on her Make a Difference Day star.

Had his booth always been close to Sea View Scoops?

"I know it's hard waiting, smelling those delicious waffle cones," she said, wiping the drool off his booth.

As the morning went on, the crowd grew. "Paint portraits of pets. Raise money for the animals!" Sylvie said into her megaphone. "Help the dogs. Help the cats." She passed it to Sammy.

"Bugs and reptiles, too," he said.

Josh and Nick finished setting up their booth. They waved. Sylvie checked her watch. They were starting at 8:30 in the morning? *Better late than never*, she thought. And their signs looked terrific.

"Great posters!" said Sylvie. "That cursive really pops."

The day was turning out terrific. It sounded like everyone's projects were going great.

As for her project, Sylvie calculated she and Sammy would make so much money that all the animals in the world would be set for life. They could move into fancy apartments. Eat from crystal bowls. Get their fur styled daily, and claws buffed and shined.

In fact, she was sure they'd collect so much money that they would need a bigger donation jar. Sylvie ran into the flower shop, and the cashier agreed to lend her a supersized vase.

Back outside, a familiar voice greeted her. "Your pink paint is running low."

Sylvie turned. Boxes of garbage bags were piled high in her ex-best friend's arms. Just waiting for all those leaves. Mount Camilla. Sylvie's cheeks felt warm.

But then a movement made her turn and glance at the dog, her big star, sitting proudly on his pillows. Was he even closer to Sea View Scoops?

She remembered her vision of dogs and their crystal bowls. No, Sylvie would not let Camilla upset her. Not now. Not on Make a Difference Day.

"OK, thanks. I'll pick up more," Sylvie replied. "Getting started on your leaf collecting?"

"I started hours ago," Camilla replied. "I just needed more bags. I might set a world record. Come to think of it, I'd better go back right now and buy even more."

Sylvie squeezed her supersized vase-donation-jar tight. *Really?* she thought. "Really?" she hollered as Camilla ran to the hardware shop.

Sylvie realized the art store was a few blocks away. She hoped the Paint Out would be OK on its own for a little while.

Sylvie picked up the can of paint and walked back more determined than ever to have the best project. She'd get more paintings. More sales.

"More making a difference—" Her voice trailed off when she saw the dog.

"Gah!" Sylvie screamed.

The dog stared with an ice cream covered snout. The pillows beneath him were soaked in sticky strawberry sauce.

Sylvie's eyes darted from the dog to the table, and back again. "My Paint Out! What happened to my Paint Out?"

# PAINTS OUT?

Sylvie charged for the table just a few feet away. Her mouth fell open.

The paintings were splattered in ice cream. No one would want to buy them now.

Hot chocolate syrup and warm, wet walnuts dripped down corners of some of the blank canvases. Others were covered in paint and sprinkles. People couldn't paint on them now.

Rainbow sprinkles blew in the breeze. Sylvie might never look at sprinkles the same way.

How could this have happened?

She looked around. Paintings of Henry's goldfish and two giant pandas, her parents' favorite animal, were propped up on easels. A tarantula portrait kept them company. It strongly resembled Sammy's spider, Fluffy.

They must have all been too busy painting to notice. The dog probably snuck away right under their paint-smudged noses.

The dog wagged his tail. *Seriously?*
thought Sylvie. She put down the paint.
The scent of fresh waffle cone wafted

through the air. The dog barked. Sylvie

blinked back tears.

"Sylvie?" whispered Camilla.

Sylvie looked up to find her former best friend. Camilla must have just come out of the hardware shop again.

"I'm sorry," Camilla said. Then she walked away. Sylvie's jaw dropped.

Had Camilla said something nice to her? Before Sylvie could call out to Camilla, she felt a tap on her shoulder.

She turned to see who it was. It was Sammy, just back from giving his turtle, Shelly, her eye drops. He didn't know what had happened! Sylvie knew she had to break the news.

"What in the world?" asked Sammy.

"Well," Sylvie started. But how could she tell him?

She knew Sammy had high hopes for the fancy apartments for animals. He had said they should have a gold plated terrarium for beetles and bunk beds for bearded dragons.

She took a deep breath. "I went to get more paint," she said, shaking her head. "The dog must have snuck a waffle cone sundae. My guess it was Strawberry Dreams Deluxe."

*A fabulous choice*, thought Sylvie. "Anyway, he made a run for it and wiped out everything with him. It must have happened fast."

Sammy stared at the sidewalk. Sylvie knew his dreams had just been wiped out too. "All the animals we could have helped," he said, his voice cracking.

"I know," Sylvie said. She had already investigated rocket ships for their trip into space. Those poor space animals. Who would help them now?

Sylvie slumped down in her folding chair. Sammy sat beside her.

The dog raced over and gave them each a big slobbery kiss. Sylvie noticed a small smile spread across her best friend's face.

"I'm really sorry," he said. "I think the dog is, too."

The dog bounced up and nuzzled Sylvie. He dropped a slobbery spoon into her lap and pranced over to stand beside the portrait she had painted.

In Sylvie's masterpiece, she and the dog beamed as they shared an ice cream sundae. Sylvie stared into the dog's big eyes and let out a deep breath.

"I know you couldn't help it. Sea View Scoops sundaes are delicious."

She sat up straight. "But what gave you the idea to try one?"

Sammy did a double take, looking at Sylvie and the dog, the sundae in Sylvie's portrait, and back again.

Then he made a strange sound, and his face seemed to search the sky. Maybe he had been researching rocket ships too. He straightened his glasses. "What if we start over?" he asked.

The dog licked Sylvie. She checked her watch. "It *is* still morning," she said, packing up their supplies. "And I did have 138 other ideas."

Sylvie folded the booth and helped her mom lift it into the trunk of the car. She flipped on her megaphone.

"People, we're taking a short break. Please visit Sea View's other wonderful Make a Difference Day projects. We're going home to regroup and come up with another plan. Stay tuned."

# CHEW TOYS, SQUEAKY TOYS, FUZZY TOYS. OH MY!

"Dog!" Sylvie cheered, back at her house.

She, Sammy, and Henry were brainstorming new ideas, and the dog had just given her the best one. She tossed the toy he had brought over.

"You're a genius!" He was such a smart and amazing dog. Sylvie wished she knew his name. Then she could praise him properly.

Sammy got up from his stool in the kitchen. He and Henry looked at each other.

"Wait. A genius?" Sammy asked.

"Yes!" Sylvie said. "The toy. We might not be able to collect money from the art sales for the animals. But we can collect toys for them. We can make a difference that way."

"Collect toys for all the animals in the world?" Sammy asked.

"Exactly!" Sylvie imagined dogs fetching frisbees, cats chasing balls of yarn, and guinea pigs playing Go Fish.

"I have an old dinosaur toy," said Henry.

Sammy's eyes brightened. "My bearded dragon, Bernice, loves dinosaurs. All dinosaur toys go to the beardies!"

"It's settled," said Sylvie. "The animal shelter people are coming to pick up the puppy anyway. They can pick up the toys then, too."

She got Henry's red wagon from the garage. Then Sylvie, Sammy, and Henry got to work. They took turns pulling the wagon.

They practiced their pitch. "Happy Make a Difference Day!" said Henry. "We're collecting new or gently used toys for dogs, cats, and all the animals in the world."

"Especially bugs and reptiles," added Sammy.

"Then possibly the space animals," Sylvie prompted.

Despite having to stop for snacks, lunch, and to give Sammy's cat his anti-itch ointment, the mission was a success.

Back at home, Sylvie admired their

haul. After a long day of "pounding the pavement," as Mr. Wolf called it, Sylvie and her team had collected the best donations ever.

Chew toys. Squeaky toys. Fuzzy toys. Plus, people donated old towels, water bowls, collars, and leashes.

Sylvie's dad walked onto the patio. "Nice job! I just heard from the animal shelter. They'll be here in an hour."

"We'll get everything ready," said Sylvie. When they stacked the toys in one pile, it looked big. Like a mountain. Sylvie grinned from ear to ear. Mount Sylvie!

The dog stared at Mount Sylvie. Sylvie patted him as they marveled at Mount Sylvie's splendor together.

The dog barked at a tennis ball. Sylvie supposed she could spare one toy. She bent down and pulled it out for him.

But as she looked at the pile of toys, she noticed a tiny smudge on a chew toy. A little smear on a squeaky toy. A small splotch on a fuzzy toy.

"Oh no!" Sylvie picked up a smudged toy. She scrubbed it with the corner of her shirt. *That only made it worse,* she thought. "This won't do. We've got to clean everything. We can't give the animals dirty toys."

Sylvie checked her watch. They had twenty minutes. "We need more cleaning power," she said, scanning the yard.

Just then, the dog charged over with a mouthful of grass. That gave Sylvie an idea. She raced to the side of the house and returned with the garden hose.

"I'm not sure about this," said Sammy.

"It's fine," Sylvie replied. "We can always put the toys in the dryer."

Henry grabbed for the hose. "Water fight!"

Sylvie blocked her brother. She turned the sprayer to mist setting.

"No water fight. We've got to be careful. Too much water will make the toys muddy. Plus, we would never want to waste water." Surely Henry remembered her water conservation-themed sixth birthday party?

Sylvie misted the toys and shook off the extra water. Sammy and Henry grabbed towels and dried them more. They didn't even need the dryer.

The toys shimmered. They sparkled. Henry and Sammy ran to get some boxes.

Sylvie took a moment to herself with the new-and-improved Mount Sylvie. She stepped back for a better view. "Stellar!"

It was breathtaking. It was perfect.

It was raining? Sylvie held up her hands. No, it couldn't be!

She spun around in every direction. No rain at Mr. Wolf's. No rain at Camilla's. Sylvie's eyes searched the sky. Clear blue. No gray. No clouds.

She looked back at Mount Sylvie. Rain and more rain. Mud splattered everywhere.

"What on earth is going on?" yelled Sylvie.

*SNAP!* She swung her head around. Thunder? Lightning?

But no. She had not heard thunder. She had not seen lightning. She had not felt rain.

The rain and the sounds came from something else—a gushing green garden hose. It was firmly in the mouth of a soaking wet puppy. And it was aimed squarely at Mount Sylvie.

# THE QUESTION

The dog galloped past Sylvie. He bit down on the handle and flooded the mountain of toys.

"Stop!" Sylvie screamed. He didn't stop. He inched closer. He clomped through puddles and sprayed the toys.

"No!" Sylvie shouted.

The toys would be so soggy and dirty the animal shelter would never want them. No one would.

But the dog kept going. If Sylvie didn't know better, she might have thought he was doing it on purpose.

She hurried to turn off the spigot. The water stopped. The dog rolled in the mud.

Sylvie collapsed on the porch step. It was official. She and Sammy wouldn't make the biggest difference ever. They wouldn't make any difference at all.

It would definitely have been time to throw in the towel—except Sylvie couldn't even do that. The towels were all dripping in mud!

Sylvie heard the sound of tires on the driveway. She looked up and saw a white truck with a *Sea View Animal Shelter* sticker rolling toward her.

Sylvie's dad stepped outside. Sammy and Henry ran past him, carrying boxes for the toys.

"Sylvie," her dad said, "the animal shelter is going to love everything you kids collected!"

Sylvie was about to tell her dad what had happened. But she didn't need to. She could tell he could see for himself. "Oh, Sylvie," he said. "I'm so sorry."

After the animal shelter people parked, Sylvie explained what had happened. "Usually he's super sweet. Maybe even the best puppy ever."

The dog sidled up to her, gnawing on a hair clip. "Even if he likes to eat my hair clips. And lists. And especially my snickerdoodles."

Henry started to build a mud castle where Mount Sylvie had been.

Sylvie felt her cheeks warm. "But I don't know what happened today.

"First, he completely messed up our Paint Out. And then he tried to get all the toys and everything else wet and filthy so we would have nothing to give. It's like he wanted to ruin Make a Difference Day."

Sammy shook his head. "He really did it this time."

"Hmm," said her dad, patting Sylvie on the back. Then he walked over to the muddy puppy. The dog flipped onto his back and wagged his wet tail.

After a minute, her dad made a funny face. The same face he made when he discovered Sylvie donated every pair of his sneakers to the school shoe drive the night before his marathon. Or when Sylvie pledged the entire kitchen pantry to the community food bank the day before Thanksgiving.

Then, the most unbelievable and unforgivable thing happened. Sylvie's dad rubbed the dog's belly.

"Dad!" said Sylvie.

"Dad!" said Henry.

"Mr. Schwartz!" said Sammy.

"Dad, you can't reward him for this behavior!" Sylvie said.

Sylvie's dad pressed his lips together. It almost seemed as if he was trying not to laugh. He walked over and placed his hands on Sylvie's shoulders. "Kids, I think the dog just wanted to help."

"What?" cried Sylvie.

"He saw you cleaning the toys. He tried to join in," said her dad.

"He tried to help?" asked Henry.

"Looks that way."

Henry giggled. Sammy giggled. The animal shelter people giggled. The dog barreled over and smacked kisses on everyone. Everyone but Sylvie.

Sylvie had stepped back. She didn't know how to feel. But she didn't feel like giggling. So the dog might have been trying to help. A lot of good it did.

The people from the shelter started talking with her dad. They must have been going over arrangements about taking the dog. Sylvie didn't need to be around for that.

She peeked inside the truck. She wasn't the only curious one. The dog brushed past her and jumped in.

A wire cage rested in the back. How could such a big puppy fit into such a tiny cage?

The dog sniffed around. His nose went down. His ears went down. His tail went down. For the first time, his tail lost its wag. His slobbery kisses dried up.

Forgetting how upset she felt, Sylvie knelt and scratched behind his ears. He almost seemed as scared as the day she found him.

"You'll be OK," she whispered. The dog gave Sylvie a kiss. It felt warm and tickly like always. He circled her legs and sat on her feet.

"I'll let you take the leatherback sea turtle and any of the other endangered stuffies you want."

The dog's ears perked up. He dashed to the house. Sylvie followed.

The dog flew inside and barked at a fly. It would be quiet without him. What if he *had* been trying to help?

Sylvie took one last look at the truck. The nice shelter people would take good care of him. Still, she didn't feel certain the dog would be happy.

Suddenly, something struck her. Maybe the dog belonged somewhere else.

Was this the way Sylvie could make the biggest difference of all? She raced outside and blurted the question to her parents.

# SNICKERS SCHWARTZ

Sylvie bounced. "So can we?" she asked. She already had so many great ideas for names.

Sylvie's parents looked at each other. Her mom kissed her forehead. "It would be a wonderful thing to do," she said.

"It's a big responsibility," said her dad. "But—"

*But?* thought Sylvie. *But?* That could not be good.

She had to convince them. She clasped her hands together. "Please! I know it's a lot," Sylvie interrupted. "Sammy spends hours taking care of Shelly, and she's just a little turtle."

"Good point," said her dad. "But—"

*Oh no!* She had to turn this around. Plus, her dad had a clipboard! It must have been the papers to send the dog to the shelter. She had no time!

"But," Sylvie interrupted. "Sammy gets to watch Shelly swim and climb. And he says no one is a better listener."

Her parents nodded.

She went on. She had to prove she was up to the task. "I don't have eight pets to take care of like Sammy. But I do have one Henry. And being Henry's big sister is no small task."

Sylvie's dad's mouth crinkled to a smile. "Is that so?" he asked.

Her mom winked. "You are a great helper. And you've done a terrific job with all your Make a Difference Day responsibilities."

Sylvie felt her heart skip. "So?" she asked. "Does that mean yes? Can we adopt him?"

"It's a big responsibility." Sylvie's dad handed over the clipboard. *"But* we know you can do it."

Sylvie looked to see the words she had been hoping for. "Yes?" she asked, reading the *Pet Adoption Agreement.* "Yes!"

Sylvie couldn't believe it. She'd found the most stellar Make a Difference Day idea. She filled out the forms in her best cursive. And with that, the dog officially became family.

Sylvie hugged Snickers as tight as she could. He offered a slobbery kiss in return. Sylvie giggled. "You know what? Maybe we can make a difference for all the other animals, too."

Sylvie raced to the car, pulled the booth from the trunk, and dragged it onto the lawn.

She grabbed paint and instructed her team to make a few changes. Henry painted "Kissing Booth." Sammy painted "Donations Support Sea View Animal Shelter." Sylvie painted "Starring Snickers Schwartz."

The dog went back to his position. He was the star, after all.

Even if it was harder to see him without the pillows. Unfortunately the pillows were still soaked in strawberry sauce. And for some reason, Sylvie wasn't allowed to take others.

It was dark, so Sylvie's parents set up some extra lights. Sylvie powered up her megaphone. A crowd gathered. Josh and Nick were still a carrying "Free Hugs!!" sign.

And that gave Sylvie an idea.

She grabbed Josh, Nick, and their other friends. They huddled in Sylvie's garage and she explained her new plan.

The kids carried out more tables. More chairs. More megaphones. Soon, the Schwartzes' lawn had become a one-stop shop for everyone's Make a Difference Day dreams.

Sylvie had even found a use for the Paint Out portraits. After all, splatter art could be very cool.

"It's Make a Difference Day *Night*," Sylvie announced to the crowd. "Let's get with the program, people."

Mr. Wolf was first in line. "Tremendous job," he said. "Sylvie, you're our Sea View Star."

Ms. Martin waited behind him. "Way to go!" she said.

Sylvie sparkled.

Sammy brushed Snickers's ears between customers. "Looking good," Sylvie said.

She turned to the crowd and spoke into her megaphone. "Get your good night kiss from Sea View's newest resident!" she yelled. She passed the megaphone to Sammy.

"Support the animal shelter!" he said, and passed the megaphone to Henry.

"Sylvie, is it snack time yet?" Henry

shouted straight into the local news camera now on the scene.

The kissing booth was a huge success. Sylvie and her team raised tons of money. Their friends' projects were huge hits too. By the end of the night, it seemed as if everyone in town had come by.

*Everyone except for one person*, Sylvie thought. She put down her megaphone, and she snuck into Ms. Kay's yard.

Camilla was still raking. She had piled the bursting-full bags on the lawn. Sylvie had never seen so many bags! But

Camilla didn't look as pleased as Sylvie expected.

"Ms. Kay is going to be so happy," said Sylvie.

Camilla puffed out a puffball on her sweater. She shrugged. "I got them all," she replied. "You don't need to help."

Ms. Kay's leaves were bagged. But Sylvie realized she could help Camilla another way.

"We're celebrating Make a Difference Day *Night*. Want to come?" she asked.

No response.

She went on. "Ms. Martin is there.

Maybe she'll even give you some extra credit?"

A smile spread across Camilla's face. She let her rake fall.

Sylvie took Camilla's hand. The girls crossed the tree line and ran into the Schwartzes' lawn together.

When Camilla saw the kissing booth, she stopped suddenly. She made a funny face, dropped Sylvie's hand, muttered something, and sped off.

*What now?* thought Sylvie.

Moments later, Camilla returned, carrying her biggest bags of leaves. She pointed to the barely-there Snickers. "Maybe this can help?"

"Stellar!" said Sylvie, placing the bags to prop up her new pet.

Camilla complained that the dog needed a bath and "extra-strength" mouthwash. Sylvie saw her giggle when she got her puppy kisses. Sylvie didn't say anything, but she let Camilla take an extra turn, for free.

At the end of the night, Sylvie gathered with her team.

"Stellar job," she said. "Now get some sleep. We've got only 364 more days

until the next Make a Difference Day.

Better start planning!"

## MAKE A DIFFERENCE DAY

is one of the largest national days of community service. Celebrated on the fourth Saturday of October, thousands of volunteers unite in a common mission to improve the lives of others.

For more information, please visit: http://www.pointsoflight.org/make-a-difference-day